THE SERIES

Welcome to Alola!

Adapted by Maria S. Barbo

©2017 The Pokémon Company International. ©1997-2017 Nintendo, Creatures, GAME FREAK, TV Tokyo, ShoPro, JR Kikaku. TM, ® Nintendo.

Published by Scholastic Inc., *Publishers since 1920.* SCHOLASTIC and associated logos are trademarks and/or registered trademarks of Scholastic Inc.

ISBN 978-1-338-14864-0

12 11 10 9 8 7 6 5 4 3   17 18 19 20 21

Printed in the U.S.A.   40

First printing 2017

SCHOLASTIC INC.

"Yippee!" shouted Ash. "Full throttle, Sharpedo!"

"*Pika!*" Pikachu agreed.

Ash and Pikachu were on vacation in the Alola region. And it was awesome!

They rode the waves on a Sharpedo.
They dove to the bottom of the ocean.
They even saw a Pyukumuku.
Ash could not wait to tell his mom about
all the cool new Pokémon he had met!

"Race you to the hotel!" Ash told Pikachu.

"*Pika pi!*" Pikachu zipped ahead of Ash.

"You won't beat me!" Ash said.

Ash ran so fast he did not see the Litten in his path. He stomped right on its tail.

"Sorry!" Ash said.

But the Fire Cat Pokémon didn't hear him.

It spat a flaming hairball at Ash's face!

Ash hurried to meet his mom and her Mr. Mime. They rode to town in a Tauros taxi.

"This is the best ever!" Ash said.

"Later, we can visit the Pokémon School," his mom said.

"Wow, look at that cool Grubbin!" Ash said. Ash and Pikachu went to take a closer look. The Bug-type Pokémon pinched Ash's nose. Then it raced away.

"Ouch!" Ash cried. "Let's catch it, Pikachu!"

"Hey, slow down!" Ash called.
He and Pikachu chased Grubbin into a
forest.

"Where are we?" Ash asked.
Ash and Pikachu were lost!

Ash and Pikachu did not mind being lost. There were so many cool Pokémon to find!

"Is that a Bewear?" Ash asked. "Look, it's waving!"

The Strong Arm Pokémon swung its paw at a tree.

Then Bewear spun in a circle and
chopped down two more trees.

"Wah!" Ash screamed. "Pikachu, move it!"

"*Pika pika pika!*" cried Pikachu.

Ash and Pikachu ran out of the forest.

They spotted a boy riding a Charizard up in the sky.

"Let's follow it!" Ash said.

"*Pika!*" Pikachu agreed.

Soon Ash and Pikachu reached a place full of
Trainers and Pokémon. They saw a Popplio, a
Bounsweet, and a Togedemaru.

"Whoa!" Ash said. "So many Pokémon!"
He jumped over a fence—right into the path of
three charging Tauros!

"Welcome to the Pokémon School," one
rider said. "I'm Mallow. I'll show you around."
She led Ash and Pikachu into a classroom.
    "Pokémon and students study together at
our school," Mallow said.

Ash ran to the window and leaned out.
"Wow, this place is cool," he said.
"Hey, who are those guys?"

Ash watched as three bullies taunted a boy and his Charizard.

"They're part of Team Skull," Mallow told him. "They are always trying to pick a fight."

"*Pika.*" Pikachu scowled.

One of Team Skull's thugs got in the boy's face. "Kiawe, if you can beat us in a Pokémon battle, maybe we'll let you walk away."

"But if we beat you, then your Charizard belongs to us!" said another.

Charizard growled.

Ash ran out onto the field. Three against one was not fair.

"You are cowards!" he said. "I'll fight, too."

"*Pika pi!*" Pikachu was ready to defend its friend.

"Those guys are dangerous, Ash!" Mallow
warned.

"And I don't need any help," said Kiawe.

But it was too late.

Team Skull called to their Pokémon.

"Salandit, show them your strength with Venoshock!"

"Yungoos, use Bite!"

"Zubat, Leech Life!"

"Pikachu," Ash called. "I choose you! Use Quick Attack!"

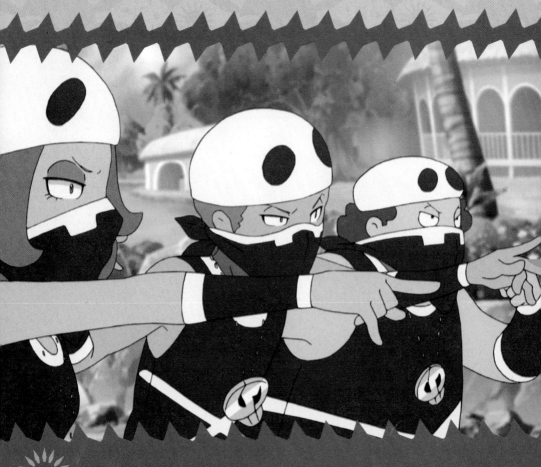

Pikachu blasted Team Skull's Pokémon with an electric charge.

Salandit fell to the ground.

"That was fast!" said Kiawe.

"*Pika! Pika!*" said Pikachu.

"Turtonator, come on out!" Kiawe called.

"Wow, totally awesome!" said Ash. "A Fire-and-Dragon type."

Turtonator blocked Yungoos with its shell. Its spines exploded on contact.

And so did Team Skull's Pokémon!

"Whoa!" said Ash. "The Pokémon in Alola are super cool!"

But Team Skull wasn't done fighting.

"Quick, Salandit, use Flame Burst!" cried one of the thugs.

Salandit used their tails to fling flames at Pikachu.

"Pikachu, use Thunderbolt!" cried Ash.

"*Pikachuuuuuuuuu!*" Pikachu charged up its cheeks.

ZAP! Pikachu shocked the Salandit until they were unable to battle.

"Way to go!" Ash shouted.

"All right, Turtonator, Inferno Overdrive," said Kiawe. "Let's go!"

Turtonator was ready to fight. "*Turt!*"

"Uh-oh!" Team Skull knew what was about to happen.

"Could it be *the* move?" the thugs asked.

The Z-Ring on Kiawe's wrist began to glow. A flame grew all around him.

"Like the great mountain of Akala, become a raging fire and burn!" he cried.

"*Tur. To. Nator!*" Turtonator blasted the bullies with a giant fireball.

"No fair!" Team Skull shouted as they hurried away. "We won't forget this!"

"What was that?" Ash asked.

"Z-Moves are passed down in the Alola region," Kiawe said.

"Wow!" said Ash. "This place is so cool!" He wanted to become a Pokémon Master. And this was a great place to learn!

"Hey, who's that Pokémon?" Ash pointed to a yellow Pokémon with an orange crest on its head. He was the only one who could see it.

"That sounds like Tapu Koko, Guardian of Melemele Island," Mallow said.

That night, Tapu Koko came to see Ash again.

"Is there something you want to tell me?" Ash asked.

The Guardian Pokémon nodded. It gave Ash a Z-Ring just like the one Kiawe wore.

Ash put the band on his wrist.
It made him feel powerful. Like a new
adventure was about to begin.

Ash knew what he had to do.
He and Pikachu would stay in Alola.
They wanted to study at the Pokémon School.
There was so much to learn!
Ash did not want to miss a thing.